# Lucky

## Gus Clarke

Andersen Press • London

Copyright © 2005 by Gus Clarke

The rights of Gus Clarke to be identified as the author and illustrator of this work

have been asserted by him in accordance with the Copyright, Designs and Patents Act, 1988.

First published in Great Britain in 2005 by Andersen Press Ltd., 20 Vauxhall Bridge Road, London SW1V 2SA.

Published in Australia by Random House Australia Pty., 20 Alfred Street, Milsons Point, Sydney, NSW 2061.

All rights reserved. Colour separated in Italy by Fotoriproduzioni Grafiche, Verona.

Printed and bound in Italy by Grafiche AZ, Verona.

10   9   8   7   6   5   4   3   2   1

British Library Cataloguing in Publication Data available.

ISBN  1 84270 425 7

This book has been printed on acid-free paper

Hello. I'm Lucky.

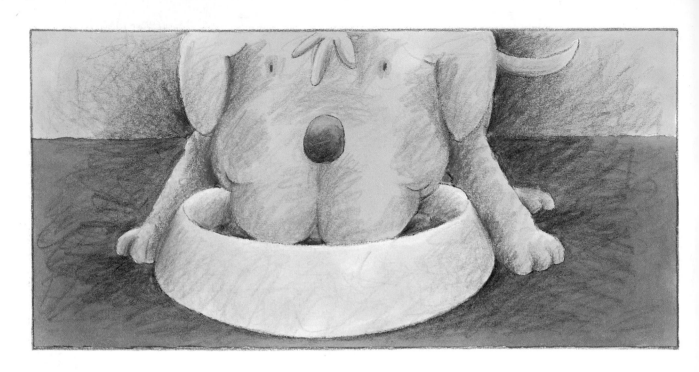

I've got plenty to eat,

a roof over my head,

a comfortable bed

and lots of friends.

We all have.

We all came here for different reasons.

I'm not sure why I came, but I'm glad I did.

Bernard hoped he wouldn't be here long. But he knows he won't be going home now.

Jim and Edna look after us. They're very good. Sometimes they bring people round to see if we'd like to go and live with them.

Bernard says he's not found the right person yet.

But Molly did.

And so did Spike.

Here come some more people. I wonder if Bernard will like these ones.

No. But Buster did!

Poor Bernard. I know he'd like to find someone to go home with.
He's getting a bit too old for all this excitement.

I've had an idea! I'll tell the others. They're sure to understand.

Here they come. Chins up, Bernard! Give them a smile.

That's nice!

Oh well, fingers crossed . . .

Well done, Walter.

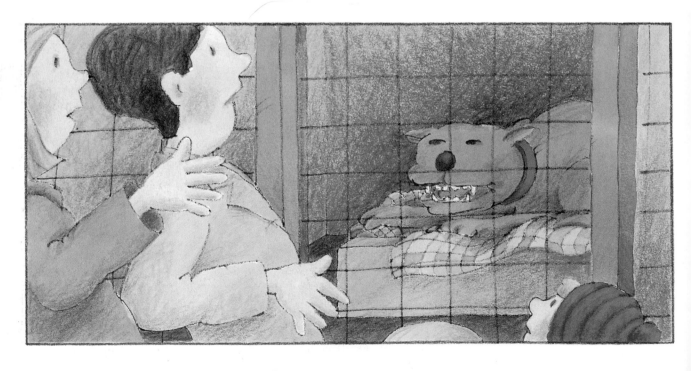

Nice one, Nick.

Good girl, Gertie.

Bad boy, Ben. (That's brilliant!)

I think it worked!

Goodbye, Bernard. We'll miss you.
I wonder if *I'll* ever find someone.

But then again . . .

. . . I might just stay!

# Other picture books by Gus Clarke:

## . . . Along Came Eric

'Brilliantly funny and perceptive story.'
*Books for Keeps*

## Betty's Not Well Today

'A wealth of detail to enjoy and talk about . . .
Certainly a book I would recommend.'
*Nursery World*

## Eddie and Teddy

'Small, concentrated and brilliant.'
Anthony Browne